Absolutely Positively

ALEXANDER

This collection is for Mickey Choate and his Alexander

—J.V.

JUDITH VIORST

Absolutely Positively
ALEXANDER

THE COMPLETE STORIES

illustrated by RAY CRUZ *and* Robin Preiss Glasser *in the style of Ray Cruz*

ATHENEUM BOOKS FOR YOUNG READERS

Atheneum Books for Young Readers
An imprint of Simon & Schuster Children's Publishing Division
1230 Avenue of the Americas
New York, New York 10020

Book design by Nina Barnett

The text of this book is set in Plantin.

First Edition
Printed in the United States of America
10   9   8   7   6   5   4   3

ISBN 0-689-81773-8
Library of Congress Catalog Card Number: 97-71981

Contents

Dear Reader,

Bad things happen—a lot—to Alexander. He has this really, really rotten day. He used to be rich but now he only has bus tokens. And his mom and dad are making him leave his best friend Paul and his soccer team and move somewhere a thousand miles away.
Yes, bad things happen—a lot—to Alexander.

It's true that whenever he's sad or mad he wants to leave—he wants to go to Australia. But most of the time he likes it right where he is. So he's going to barricade his door, or live by himself in a tree house, or hide in the pickle barrel at Friendly's Market. One thing's for sure: He is not—absolutely not, positively not—he is not (Do you hear him? He means it!) going to move.

But sometimes, whether they like it or not, boys (and girls) have to move. And sometimes they wake up with gum in their hair. And sometimes, even though they mean to save up their money to buy a walkie-talkie, they spend it on dumb stuff like a one-eyed bear. And sometimes they have brothers (or sisters) who make them fall in the mud, or call them puke-face.

All these things and more—a lot more—happen to Alexander. I write about them in the stories in this book. So sit down and take a look if you've ever been scrunched or smushed, if you've ever been scolded or picked on, if you've ever thrown a ball through a window pane, if you've ever spilled a goldfish bowl on your teacher, if nobody pays attention when you complain, if you're having—Do you hear me?— an absolutely, positively, terrible, horrible, no good, very bad day.

Judith Viorst, Alexander's mom

Alexander and the Terrible, Horrible, No Good, Very Bad Day

For Robert Lescher, with love and thanks

I went to sleep with gum in my mouth and now there's gum in my hair and when I got out of bed this morning I tripped on the skateboard and by mistake I dropped my sweater in the sink while the water was running and I could tell it was going to be a terrible, horrible, no good, very bad day.

3

At breakfast Anthony found a Corvette Sting Ray car kit in
his breakfast cereal box and Nick found a Junior Undercover
Agent code ring in his breakfast cereal box but in my
breakfast cereal box all I found was breakfast cereal.

I think I'll move to Australia.

In the car pool Mrs. Gibson let Becky have a seat by the window. Audrey and Elliott got seats by the window too. I said I was being scrunched. I said I was being smushed. I said, if I don't get a seat by the window I am going to be carsick. No one even answered.

I could tell it was going to be a terrible, horrible, no good,
very bad day.

At school Mrs. Dickens liked Paul's picture of the sailboat better than my picture of the invisible castle.

At singing time she said I sang too loud. At counting time she said I left out sixteen. Who needs sixteen?
I could tell it was going to be a terrible, horrible, no good, very bad day.

I could tell because Paul said I wasn't his best friend anymore. He said that Philip Parker was his best friend and that Albert Moyo was his next best friend and that I was only his third best friend.

I hope you sit on a tack, I said to Paul. I hope the next time you get a double-decker strawberry ice-cream cone the ice cream part falls off the cone part and lands in Australia.

There were two cupcakes in Philip Parker's lunch bag and Albert got a Hershey bar with almonds and Paul's mother gave him a piece of jelly roll that had little coconut sprinkles on the top. Guess whose mother forgot to put in dessert?

It was a terrible, horrible, no good, very bad day.

That's what it was, because after school my mom took us all
to the dentist and Dr. Fields found a cavity just in me. Come
back next week and I'll fix it, said Dr. Fields.

Next week, I said,
I'm going to Australia.

On the way downstairs the elevator door
closed on my foot and while we were
waiting for my mom to go get the car
Anthony made me fall where it was
muddy and then when I started crying
because of the mud Nick said I was a
crybaby and

16

while I was punching Nick for saying crybaby my mom came back with the car and scolded me for being muddy and fighting.

I am having a terrible, horrible, no good, very bad day, I told everybody. No one even answered.

So then we went to the shoestore to buy some sneakers. Anthony chose white ones with blue stripes. Nick chose red ones with white stripes. I chose blue ones with red stripes but then the shoe man said, We're all sold out. They made me buy plain old white ones, but they can't make me wear them.

21

When we picked up my dad at his office he said I couldn't play with his copying machine, but I forgot. He also said to watch out for the books on his desk, and I was careful as could be except for my elbow. He also said don't fool around with his phone, but I think I called Australia. My dad said please don't pick him up anymore.

It was a terrible, horrible, no good, very bad day.

There were lima beans for dinner and I hate limas.

There was kissing on TV and I hate kissing.

My bath was too hot, I got soap in my eyes, my marble went down the drain, and I had to wear my railroad-train pajamas. I hate my railroad-train pajamas.

When I went to bed Nick took back the pillow he said I could keep and the Mickey Mouse night light burned out and I bit my tongue.

The cat wants to sleep with Anthony, not with me.

It has been a terrible, horrible, no good, very bad day.

My mom says some days are like that.

Even in Australia.

Alexander, Who Used to Be Rich Last Sunday

To the boys' Grandma Betty and Grandpa Louie Viorst

It isn't fair that my brother Anthony has two dollars and three quarters and one dime and seven nickels and eighteen pennies.

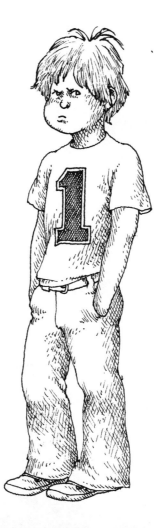

It isn't fair that my brother Nicholas has one dollar and two quarters and five dimes and five nickels and thirteen pennies.

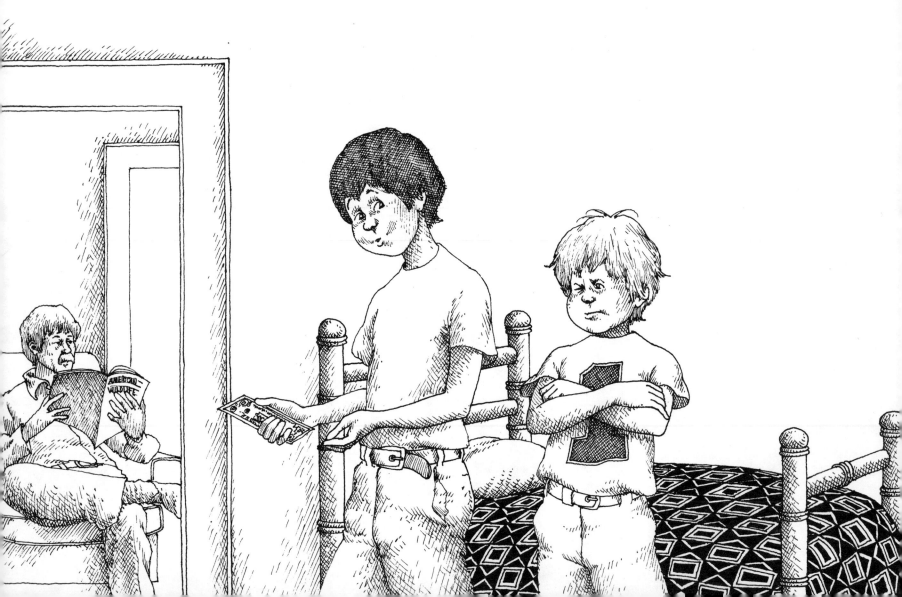

It isn't fair because what I've got is...bus tokens.

And most of the time what I've mostly got is...bus tokens.

And even when I'm very rich, I know that pretty soon what I'll have is...bus tokens.

I know because I used to be rich. Last Sunday.

Last Sunday Grandma Betty and Grandpa Louie came to visit from New Jersey.
They brought lox because my father likes to eat lox. They brought
plants because my mother likes to grow plants.

They brought a dollar for me and a dollar for Nick and a dollar for Anthony because—Mom says it isn't nice to say this—we like money.

A lot. Especially me.

My father told me to put the dollar away to pay for college.

He was kidding.

Anthony told me to use the dollar to go downtown to a store and buy
a new face. Anthony stinks.

Nicky said to take the dollar and bury it in the garden and in a week a dollar tree would grow. Ha ha ha.

Mom said if I really want to buy a walkie-talkie, save my money.

Saving money is hard.

Because last Sunday, when I used to be rich, I went to Pearson's Drug Store and got bubble gum. And after the gum stopped tasting good, I got more gum. And after that gum stopped tasting good, I got more gum. And even though I told my friend David I'd sell him all the gum in my mouth for a nickel, he still wouldn't buy it.

Good-bye fifteen cents.

Last Sunday, when I used to be rich, I bet that I could hold my breath till 300. Anthony won. I bet that I could jump from the top of the stoop and land on my feet. Nicky won.

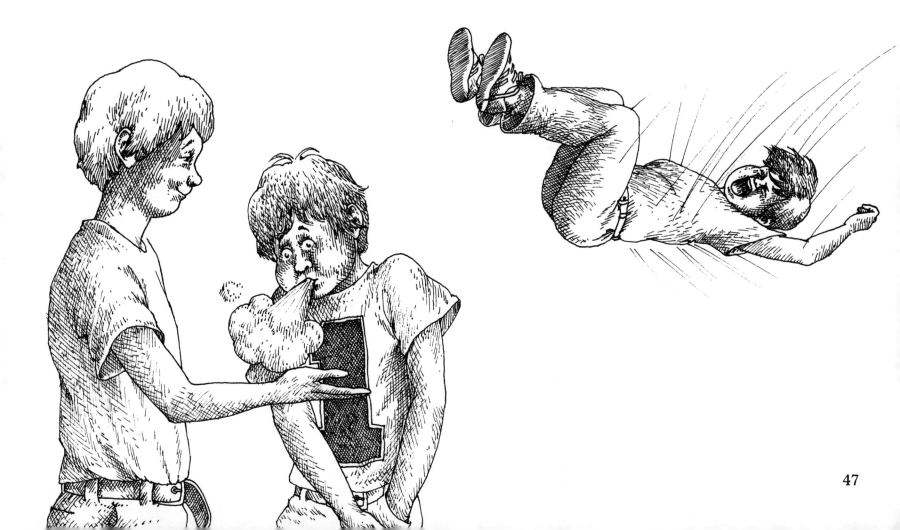

I bet that I could hide this purple marble in my hand,
and my mom would never guess which hand I was hiding it in.
I didn't know that moms made children pay.

Good-bye another fifteen cents.

I absolutely was saving the rest of my money. I positively was saving the rest of my money. Except that Eddie called me up ánd said that he would rent me his snake for an hour. I always wanted to rent his snake for an hour.

Good-bye twelve cents.

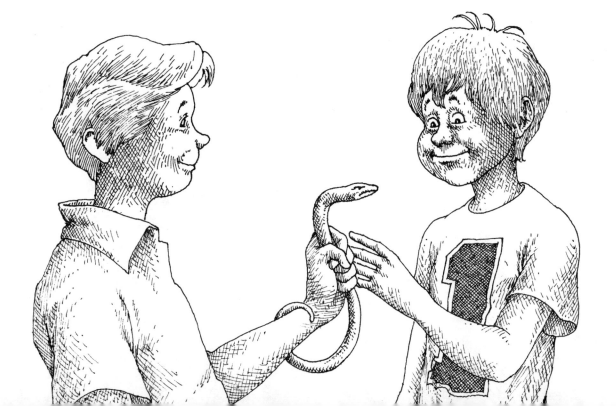

Anthony said when I'm ninety-nine I still won't have enough for
a walkie-talkie. Nick said I'm too dumb to be let loose. My father said
that there are certain words a boy can never say, no matter how ratty
and mean his brothers are being. My father fined me five cents
each for saying them.

Good-bye dime.

Last Sunday, when I used to be rich, by accident I flushed three cents
down the toilet. A nickel fell through a crack when I walked on my hands.
I tried to get my nickel out with a butter knife and also
my mother's scissors.

Good-bye eight cents.

And the butter knife.

And the scissors.

Last Sunday, when I used to be rich, I found this chocolate candy bar just sitting there. I rescued it from being melted or smushed. Except the way I rescued it from being melted or smushed was that I ate it. How was I supposed to know it was Anthony's?

Good-bye eleven cents.

I absolutely was saving the rest of my money. I positively was saving the rest of my money. But then Nick did a magic trick that made my pennies vanish in thin air. The trick to bring them back he hasn't learned yet.

Good-bye four cents.

Anthony said that even when I'm 199, I still won't have enough for a walkie-talkie. Nick said they should lock me in a cage. My father said that there are certain things a boy can never kick, no matter how ratty and mean his brothers are being. My father made me pay five cents for kicking it.

Good-bye nickel.

Last Sunday, when I used to be rich, Cathy around the corner had a garage sale. I positively only went to look. I looked at a half-melted candle. I needed that candle. I looked at a bear with one eye. I needed that bear. I looked at a deck of cards that was perfect except for no seven of clubs and no two of diamonds. I didn't need that seven or that two.

Good-bye twenty cents.

Garage Sale
neet bargens

CATHY, prop.

I absolutely was saving the rest of my money. I positively was saving the rest of my money. I absolutely positively was saving the rest of my money. Except I needed to get some money to save.

I tried to make a tooth fall out—I could put it under my pillow and get a quarter. No loose teeth.

I looked in Pearson's telephone booths for nickels and dimes that people sometimes forget. No one forgot.

I brought some non-returnable bottles down to Friendly's Market.
Friendly's Market wasn't very friendly.

I told my grandma and grandpa to come back soon.

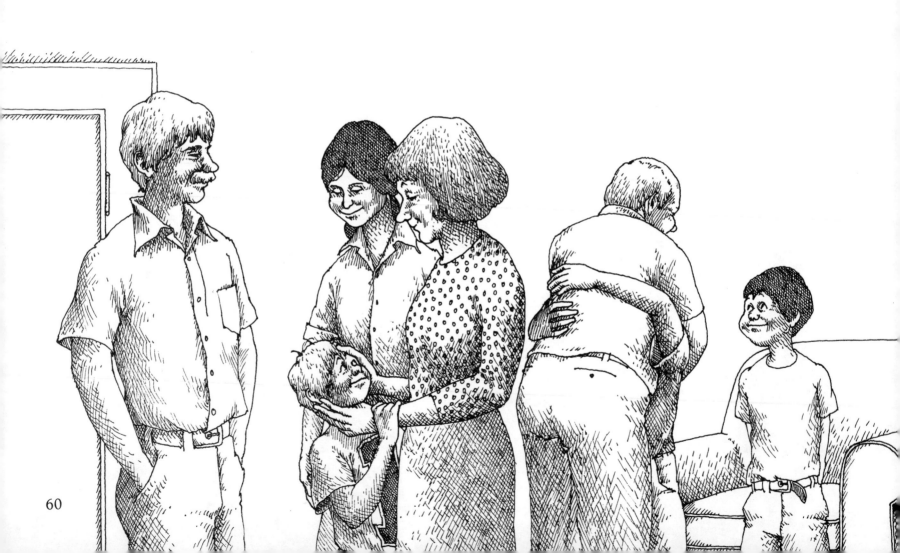

Last Sunday, when I used to be rich, I used to have a dollar. I do not have a dollar any more. I've got this dopey deck of cards. I've got this one-eyed bear. I've got this melted candle.

And…some bus tokens.

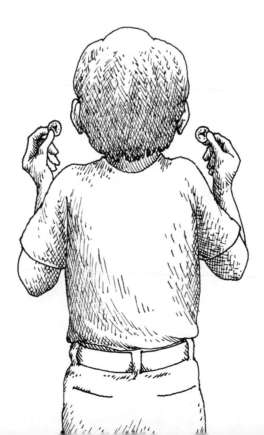

Alexander, Who's Not (Do you hear me? I mean it!) Going to Move

For Miranda Rachel Viorst

—J.V.

For my sister Erica, who has always been there for me

—R.P.G.

They can't make me pack my baseball mitt or my I LOVE DINOSAURS
sweatshirt or my cowboy boots. They can't make me pack my ice skates,
my jeans with eight zippers, my compass, my radio or my stuffed pig.
My dad is packing. My mom is packing.
My brothers Nick and Anthony are packing.

I'm not packing. I'm not going to move.

My dad says we have to move to where his new job is. That job is a thousand miles away. My mom says we have to move to where our new house is. That house is a thousand miles away. Right next door to the new house there's a boy who is Anthony's age. Down the street there's a boy the same age as Nick.

There's no one next door or down the street or maybe for a thousand miles who is my age.

I'm not—DO YOU HEAR ME? I MEAN IT!—going to move.

I'll never have a best friend like Paul again. I'll never have a great sitter like Rachel again. I'll never have my soccer team or my car pool again. I'll never have kids who know me, except my brothers, and sometimes *they* don't want to know me.

I'm not packing. I'm not going to move.

Nick says I'm a fool and should get a brain transplant. Anthony says I'm being immature. My mom and my dad say that after a while I'll get used to living a thousand miles from everything.

Never. Not ever. No way. Uh uh. N. O.

I maybe could stay here
and live with the Baldwins.
They've got a dog.

I always wanted a dog.

I maybe could stay here and live with the Rooneys. They've got six girls. They always wanted one boy.

I maybe could stay here and live with Mr. and Mrs. Oberdorfer.
They always give great treats on Halloween.

I maybe could stay here and live by myself in maybe a tree house or maybe a tent or maybe a cave.

Nick says I could live in the zoo with all the other animals.
Anthony says I'm being immature. My dad says I should take a last
look at all my special places.

I'm taking a look—but it won't be my last.

I looked at the Rooneys' roof, which I once climbed out on but then I couldn't climb back in, until the Fire Department came and helped me.
I looked at Pearson's Drug Store, where they once said my mom had to pay them eighty dollars when I threw a ball in the air that I almost caught.

I looked at the lot next to Albert's house, where I once and for all learned to tell which was poison ivy.
I looked at my school, where even Ms. Knoop, the teacher I once spilled the goldfish bowl on, said she'd miss me.

I looked at my special places where a lot of different things
happened—not just different bad but different good.
Like winning that sack race.
Like finding that flashlight.
Like spitting farther than Jack three times in a row.

Like selling so much lemonade that my dad said I would probably have to pay taxes. My dad was just making jokes about paying taxes. I wish he was just making jokes about having to move.

I'm not—DO YOU HEAR ME? I MEAN IT!—going to move.

LEMONADE
5¢
27,000,000,000 SOLD!

Internal
Revenue

Nick says I am acting like a puke-face.
Anthony says I'm being immature.
My mom says to say a last good-bye to all my special people.

I'm saying good-bye—but it won't be my last.

I said good-bye to my friends, especially Paul, who is almost like having another brother, except he doesn't say puke-face or immature.

I said good-bye to my neighbors, especially Swoozie, who is almost like having a dog, except she's the Baldwins' dog instead of mine.

I said good-bye to Rachel, who taught me to stand on my head and whistle with two fingers, but she says don't try to do both at the same time. I said good-bye to Seymour the cleaners, who—even if it's gum wrappers or an old tooth—always saves me the stuff I leave in my pockets.

I said a lot of good-byes to a lot of people and got a lot of hugs and kisses, enough hugs and kisses to last for a person's whole life. I said a lot of good-byes—except I'm staying right here. I'm not going to move.

When the movers come to put my bedroom furniture on their truck, maybe I'll barricade my bedroom door. When my dad wants to tie my bicycle to the roof rack on top of the station wagon, maybe I'll lock up my bike and bury the key. When my mom says, "Finish packing up, it's time for us to get going," maybe she'll look around and she won't see me.

I know places to hide where they'd never find me.

Like behind the racks of clothes at Seymour the cleaners.
Like underneath the piano in Eddie's basement.
Like inside the pickle barrel at Friendly's Market.
Or maybe I could hide in the weeds in the lot next to Albert's house,
now that I know how to tell which is poison ivy.

I'd rather have poison ivy than have to move.

My dad says it might take a while but I'll find a new soccer team.
He says it might take a while but I'll find boys my age.

He also says that sometimes, when a person moves away, his father might need to let him get a dog to be his friend till he makes some people friends. I think that Swoozie Two would be a good name.

My mom says it might take a while but we'll find a great sitter. She says it might take a while but we'll find a cleaners who even saves gum wrappers and old teeth. She also says that sometimes, when a person moves away, his mother might let him call his best friend long-distance.

I already know the telephone number by heart.

Paul gave me a baseball cap. Rachel gave me a backpack that glows in the dark. Mr. and Mrs. Oberdorfer gave us treats to eat for a thousand miles. Nick says if I'm lonesome in my new room all by myself, he might let me sleep with him for a little while.

Anthony says that Nick is being mature.

My dad is packing. My mom is packing.
My brothers Nick and Anthony are packing.
I don't like it, but I'm packing too.

They better not try to move anymore
when we get where we're going to go.

Because this is the last time I'll do it.
The next time they won't make me do it.
Never. Not ever. No way. Uh uh. N. O.

I'm not—DO YOU HEAR ME? I MEAN IT!—going to move.

☐ KITCHEN
☐ DINING
☐ BATH
☐ BEDROOM
☒ ALEXANDER'S NEW ROOM